Constance Finch

The Vision of a Beginner

And other Poems

Constance Finch

The Vision of a Beginner
And other Poems

ISBN/EAN: 9783337398101

Printed in Europe, USA, Canada, Australia, Japan

Cover: Foto ©Andreas Hilbeck / pixelio.de

More available books at **www.hansebooks.com**

THE VISION OF A BEGINNER

AND OTHER POEMS

BY

CONSTANCE FINCH

London

DIGBY, LONG & CO., PUBLISHERS

18 BOUVERIE STREET, FLEET STREET, E.C.

1892

CONTENTS.

———o———

	PAGE
THE VISION OF A BEGINNER,	1
ODE TO SOME HAPPY HOURS,	6
A SUMMER NIGHT'S FANCY,	9
DREAMS UPON DREAMS,	11
IT WAS LOVE'S WAY,	13
LOVE'S REQUEST,	14
APOLLO'S PRIZE,	16
ODE TO KEATS AFTER READING HIS ODE TO A NIGHTINGALE,	19
TRIOLET,	21
FALSE WORDS,	22
DOTH SLEEP MOCK LOVE?	26
A SONG OF SPRING,	28
A BALLAD OF APRIL,	29
SOMETIMES,	30
AN OCEAN FANCY,	31
IT WAS YOUR NAME!	37
A FRAGMENT,	39
MORNING AND NIGHT,	40
IF LOVE BE LIKE A ROSE,	41
TRIOLET,	43

PAGE

SONNETS—

DESIRE UNATTAINED (THREE),   44
TO A NIGHTINGALE,   47
A LONELY POPPY,   48
A THUNDERSTORM; OR, SATAN'S FALL,   49
THY LOVE AND MINE,   50
THE ELM TREE AND POOL,   51
REJECTED,   52
MONOTONY,   53
THE LEGEND OF THE OLIVE TREES,   54
WHAT'S IN A NAME?   5

LOVE'S PLAY,   56
A SIGH!   57
THE OTHER SIDE OF HEAVEN,   59

RONDELS—

'TWAS NOT IN VAIN!   62
GOOD-BYE, A LONG GOOD-BYE!   63
LOVE STOOPED AND SAID,   64
DELAY NOT SWEET!   66

THE FLIGHT OF THE MUSE,   67
WHEN THOU ART GONE!   69
ODE TO MEMORY,   70
TRIOLET,   72
IF ALL BE WELL,   73
CUPID'S CASKET,   74
ON BEING ASKED TO WRITE AN ODE TO THE DAWN,   76
HOW IS LOVE BLEST?   77
A GOOD-BYE,   79
RONDEL IN MONO-RHYME,   81
LOVE'S HEIGHT,   82
LOVE'S WAY IS BEST!   84
REVERIE ON A DEAD YEAR,   85
LOVE HEEDS NOT TIME,   87

THE VISION OF A BEGINNER

AND OTHER POEMS

THE VISION OF A BEGINNER.

THERE flashed forth music from the thousand
    swords
Of mystic warriors, who protect the sun,—
A mighty pean of triumphant words
Which woke my soul with " Rise! life has begun! "

Then from the gossamer thread most finely wove
Sparks as of crystal fire began to swing,
Till blossomed in the dark the form of Love
And smote upon that slight vibrating string.

A

Oh, how it quivered, panted, then burst forth
With mingled pain and gladness into song;
Grew overbold to test the sweet dawn's worth
Instilled with proud desire, by Love made strong.

　　*　　*　　*　　*　　*　　*

There is a rainbow wrapped about the sun,
A cloud reflects it, then can shadows be
Only without a radiance when not one
Redeeming light comes forth to set them free.

There is a hidden sweetness in all things
Unbudded, tho' the calyx holds them fast,
Voluptuous as the breath of dawning Springs
If kept secure against the chilling blast.

Infinity holds somewhere worlds of fire
Clothed with perennial life, and so each soul
Can cleave the clay that binds it and aspire
With burning strength to win a glorious goal.

So spake I to a pale disdainful Form
Which fixed my spirit with its icy stare,
"Thou hast no right to hold the Worm,
O Death, before Youth's glittering eyes.   'Tis fair

This world wherein my eyes have chanced to wake,
'Tis warmed with sunlight, drenched with beauty
   thro'
The air is full of music for my sake,
I am made strong with life, as flow'rs with dew."

But It replied, "Full of conceit is Youth,
Short-sighted, deeming land ends in the sea,
Forgetful of the other side of truth,
How many lands again beyond there be!"

My soul flies onward, and I see there come
Strange wingèd creatures, beautiful but sad,
These are the weary Loves, who have no home,
Bereft of innocence, which once they had.

The dust of many ages thickly lies
Upon the tarnished glory of their wings,
The tears of many sorrows dim their eyes,
They have forgotten the glad look of things.

If ye would only look anear, afar,
And see how tenderly the meadows smile

And mark the heavens a-light with many a star,
Ye would forget your sorrow for a while.

I will refresh you with my heart's content,
My overstore of happiness shall fill
Your empty flasks of joy with wonderment—
Taste once again enchantment's blessed rill!

But the sad Loves are weary and grown old,
They are too weary to be comforted—
Let Styx, dark stream, deep over them be rolled,
So if they may find peace among the dead.

Next do I meet a great unnumbered host
With broken lyres across their shoulders flung,
As if the soul of music they had lost,
These are the poets who have never sung.

Long since the golden mountains died in mist
Faded beyond the bourne they were so fain
To reach, alas! their lips are all unkissed
By the cold Muse they wooed, but could not gain!

Is there no hope to set their lyres in tune
When the world teems with music far and wide?
Even the swallows constant are in June,
Is hope so fleeting, cannot she abide?

They seem to smile upon my earnestness,
A smile so sad it wrings my soul with fear,
Let us pass on, "Life is a wilderness!"
They wail aloud, but Heart we will not hear.

I know the riddle is as yet unsolved,
The dawn that dreams in tender shades of grey
May ere an hour has round the world revolved,
Be melted in a watery trail away.

I know that snow grows foul upon the earth,
That roses wither, that calm seas can fret,
And death is sequel to the body's birth,
I know, but ah! remind me not just yet.

Enough to feel God's wisdom will provide
Fresh pinions for my soul, when these wings tire,
Ere the heav'ns darken, ere the lost stars slide,
Let me believe 'tis Love makes all respire!

ODE TO SOME HAPPY HOURS.

O! CRUEL hours, so fleet to fly,
  When Love entreated you to stay!
Ye heeded not his minstrelsy,
  From all his prayers ye turned away;
And flew with rosy wings, thro' skies
  As cruel as yourselves, which smile,
Revealing not to Love's sad eyes
  The heav'ns in which ye hide the while.

In vain we vowed we held you fast,
  That tho' the twilight should decline
And melt into the silent past,
  We bound you with a charm divine;
In vain—the silken fetters broke,
  Faded the fragile thong of flowers,
From a fond dream Love saddening woke,
  And found you dead, like other hours!

Is it of this the waves complain,
  When each tide bears them from the shore,
That tho' they meet so soon again,
  Time smites each foam-kiss dead at core?
The same sand gleams, yet not the same,
  Some golden pebbles slip aside,
So passion, which no pow'r can tame,
  Murmurs against Life's ebbing tide.

Why should we ask what heav'n may mean?
  'Tis surely Love from these faults free;
No parting hand shall fall between,
  No joy but lasts eternally,
The futile fears that make Love fret
  Time's finger weighing down his wings,
The shattered sweet, the vague regret,
  Heav'n will be Love, freed from these things!

Sweet hours! tho' cruel, lie at rest
  Cradled in rose leaves, wrapt in scent,
On some high world's serener breast,
  Than this, to which brief space ye lent

Such perfect rapture, dream at ease
    Secure from mortal hopes and tears,
Till Love his sign resplendent sees
    And claims you his in coming years.

Yea, tho' we mourn you lost and dead,
    Tho' yearning arms clasp only air
That sought the breathing form· instead,
    We mourn, but do not yet despair,
Love's highest hope ye cannot cheat,
    Such scent was scattered 'mong the flow'rs
Where'er ye hide, that wealth of sweet,
    Shall yet reveal you cruel hours!

A SUMMER NIGHT'S FANCY.

I FOUND a tired bee asleep,
  Within a flow'r's deep bell,
And while the night winds round it creep
Those folded petals sway to keep
  Love's treasure hidden well.

The moon sails slowly through the sky,
  The pale flow'r grows more white,
For ah! the cold moon comes to spy
What in that flow'r's heart can lie,
  To cause such sweet delight.

'Tis vain to hide thy head, oh flow'r,
  The quiv'ring petals part,
'Gainst moonbeam charms thou hast no pow'r,
Be glad that Love could dream an hour
  Secure within thy heart!

I saw you sorrowing flower weep,
   Her clinging leaves entwine
A lifeless bee, in passion deep
She crushed his tiny wings to keep
   Love's secret yet divine !

ENVOI.

Love is not Love when alien eyes
   Have found his resting-place,
The air is sacred where he sighs,
And holy are his mysteries,
   Since heav'n is Love's embrace !

DREAMS UPON DREAMS.

RONDEL.

DREAMS upon dreams I have woven together,
Breathed in their souls all my spirit's desire;
Their pinions are fashioned of one azure feather;
Yet thro' infinite space they can fly and not tire;
Beauteous as roses that bloom in fair weather,
        Dreams upon dreams!

The tears of the mist as it clasps the earth sleeping,
The breath of the foam as it kisses the wave,
The wind that complains, over hill and dale leaping,
Have striven in vain my dreams' pinions to have;
They were born of my joy, cradled yet in my
        weeping,
        Dreams upon dreams!

Dreams upon dreams, like bright angels they hover
Urging my soul to upsoar and aspire,

They would vanquish despair and hope's secret
    discover,
Tender their voices, like chords of a lyre,
Passionate, yearning, the prayers of a lover,
           Dreams upon dreams!

Dreams upon dreams, will they die with awaking?
Shuddering fade like the bloom on a rose?
When the shadows grow less and the heart ceases
    aching,
Will reality be the more lovely, who knows?
Death may hold sweeter visions than these of Life's
    making,
           Dreams upon dreams!

IT WAS LOVE'S WAY.

RONDEL.

It was Love's way in the sweet past to come
With laughing lips, where rosiest kisses grew,
And beauteous eyes be-pearled with tender dew,
Because a faithful heart was then his home ;—
Most subtle were his moods, now grave now gay,—
    It was Love's way !

And is this Love,—who comes with solemn pace ?
With wounded wings whose azure sheen is soiled ?
With restless eyes and weary yearning face,
Homeless, forlorn, tho' he has nobly toiled ?
Alas ! he comes in strange disguise to-day,—
    It is Love's way !

Love's way it shall be yet to live again,
A new proud life; but ah ! you must not blame
If the sweet lips should wear a look of pain,
Or if the once bruised wings seem frail and tame,
Remember ! and with pitying passion say,—
    It is Love's way !

LOVE'S REQUEST.

FRAGMENT.

DEAR, could I love as others do,
Contented with Love's lightest breath,
Believing love lasts longer so;
" Love me a little, and till death."

Love me a little?—ah ! no, no !
I cannot be thus satisfied;
What worth a pallid sunbeam's glow
By artificial warmth supplied ?

I feel Love is too great a Good,
Too pure a thing for us to gain
And use for life's eternal food;
The flame divine cannot remain.

I'd rather have one glimpse of heaven,
Reach the proud height, then fall to earth

Than never know the distance even
Nor all that steep ascent is worth.

Love me with passion so supreme,
Superlative, while love can last,
And I shall be content to dream
Of that one hour, tho' time be vast!

Love me with all your soul, your breath,
With all the strength that truth can prove,
Love me, not " little and till death,"
Love me, and death will die in Love!

APOLLO'S PRIZE.

In that fair land where summer ever lies
With laughing lips, in fair abandoned-wise,
Where ev'n the slightest cloudlet dare not pout,
Nor on the skies his venturous wings stretch out—
Glorious Apollo, charmed the happy hours
With magic music, till the earth blushed flow'rs,
So overcome with joy her list'ning heart.
Cupid forgot to poise his ready dart
And let a score of mortal hearts go free,
So great the magic of this minstrelsy.

The god at length grew weary, but his wit
Soon remedied this passing languid fit;
"Let now" (he said) "the happiest things alive
Come nigh, and for this wreath of laurel strive,
Which I will give to him who best displays
His guileless rapture in a song of praise."
List'ning, my heart grew strong with bold desire
To win the prize,—I tuned my trembling lyre.

But first a nightingale the challenge dared,
Confident of success, he scarcely cared
To glance upon his rivals, but began ;—
Apollo's cheek itself from red turned wan
With ecstasy, as the sweet pean thrilled
The bird's soft body, louder yet he trilled,
And as the spirit oft becomes o'erwrought
With the great sweetness of some holy thought.
Till sympathetic tears the soul lay bare,
So wept each living thing that listened there!

The next competitor, a wild sea wave,
His passionate song of happiness then gave ;
O! the wave's song was rapturous and free,
Full of the untamed music of the sea,
Yet tenderly, he made us understand
The charm that binds his kisses to the sand,
Which faithfully his yearning lips caress
With all the passion of great eagerness.

Full many a one the honour strove to win,
Birds without number, the triumphant din

B

Of waterfalls; each in his turned assayed,
At last mine also came—I grew afraid—
Speechless with great desire, before the throng
I stood, and strove to sing, alas! no song
Came from my trembling lips, my lyre away
I flung in anger at my own dismay;—
Then suddenly, just as Apollo moved
To drive me thence, the name of one I loved
Surged from my heart, it fed my lips with fire!
What need had I of help from any lyre!
Again, again I made the echoes ring
With music love alone knows how to sing.
And plucking from his brows the laurel crown,
Apollo blessed me: "Mortal, this renown
Is fairly won, justly to thee belongs
This tribute of the greatest of all songs.
A sweeter chord than any I have made,
A note whose resonance shall never fade,
A glory greater than the fire of fame,
Lies in the music of a loved one's name!"

ODE TO KEATS AFTER READING HIS ODE TO A NIGHTINGALE.

To thee, sweet Poet, turns my fainting brain
Ev'n as some streamlet lost in forest glade
Is soothed and comforted by scented shade,
So this charmed song of thine dispels my pain.
Heartsick, like thee, but sadder, out of tune
With the great world's unfathomable song,
I find no pleasure in this rich mid-June,
I hear no nightingale the shades among.

" Darkling I listen," till there fades away
This present sense of life—I panting breathe
Beside thee—see the moonlight vapours wreathe
Around the self-same landscape, soft and grey ;
Thee, not an immortal spirit, but a Form
Living my life, o'erwhelmed with love, like mine ;
A passionate heart, throbbing alive and warm—
But yet a soul, whose sorrow is divine.

The midnight breeze has also stayed awhile
Its whispering murmurs, with the trembling leaves,
Floating in dew, the rose—a scented isle—
Wond'ring inquires who so melodious grieves?
The enchanted echoes make their faint replies,
Wafting with reverent lips the sad refrain ;—
O happy air! upon whose bosom lies
Such wealth of woe, such purity of pain!

Now, that the body's selfish aims grow less,
Now, that the soul's high yearnings prompt the
    more,
When bare, unveiled I see life's littleness,
And love appears in garb unknown before,
I will arise while yet thy dream is mine,
My own weak sorrow in oblivion fling—
Let me but weep one tear thus near to thine,
And sigh my pride out while I hear thee sing!

TRIOLET.

O HAPPIEST Verses not in vain
   You wear the impress of my heart,
Fly back, then, fragile wings again
O happiest Verses not in vain,
Love wounded you with tender pain
   And made you sing of passion's smart.
O happiest Verses, not in vain
You wear the impress of my heart!

FALSE WORDS.

A POEM.

I TELL my heart a thousand times
I do not love! I do not love!
But yet the question racks my brain,
With wond'ring, wearisome refrain,
Like phantom bells with haunting chimes,
Why sigh for one thou dost not love?

How full of torture is the night
When sleep withholds the dream of thee
Yet when the vivid vision lies
Upon my closed, unconscious eyes
What grief dawns with the cruel light,
So real thy dream-kiss seemed to be!

My tutored heart, it acted well;
Thou spak'st of absence, "worlds away,'

The passionate blood leapt wild beneath,
My lips seemed cold—a flame my breath,
They knew their part, what words to say;—
I lied'! I lied! How could'st thou tell?

I lied in saying "it was best,"
I lied, pretending not to care;
As if no summer time had shed
Its blessing on the whispers said
One night of June—'twas Love's despair
Thou might'st have known, thou might'st have
    guessed!

And spring will come with soothing scent,
Woven from million violets' eyes,
And lovely swaying lilac spears,
Unmindful of my lonely tears;
The primrose ope in pale surprise,
The thrush grow bold with wonderment.

All this will be—all this will pass,
Summer and winter, autumn, spring;

Days decked with sunshine, draped with shade,
And nights in varying moons arrayed,
With countless stars far shimmering,
Thou wilt be "worlds away," alas!

This would have been, but had Love heard
Those longed-for words. Love could have borne
Such absence; faith's wings soar afar
Beyond fate's cold horizon bar,
We should have met each night each morn,
Till Love had carolled like a bird.

Cold absence bleak, this fever-glow
Of doubting, hoping, will be past—
Each day will dawn in grey the same,
And die in drear, grand skies of flame,
As if to prove how wide, how vast
The heav'ns above, the earth below!

Thou wilt not know how lips can sigh
Which said those foolish words unmoved,
Nor guess the burning tears that rise
To such unfeeling, smiling eyes;

Thou wilt not know how thou art loved,
What passion yearns to have thee nigh!

But as my untold love is strong,
As fruitless grief is vainly weak,
The human hope may grow divine
By lying lowly at Love's shrine;
The truth too great, too sweet to speak,
May bless the heart that did it wrong!

DOTH SLEEP MOCK LOVE?

RONDEL.

Doth Sleep mock Love when midnight breezes
    blend
With silent shadows by the moonbeams cast?
When the earth's limits, ev'n from end to end,
Seem knit together, distance dead at last?
Around our souls a dream of bliss is wove—
        Doth Sleep mock Love?

Not this poor brain's imaginings, ah, no!
I had not reached heav'n's pinnacle so soon,
Nor won such real ecstatic rapture so.
Endymion, dreaming mingled with the moon,
Ask of the stars, among whose smiles ye move,
        Doth Sleep mock Love?

Doth Sleep mock Love, whom Fate wounds sore
    with fears?
Can she dissemble passion's voice so well?

And feign the royal robe Love only wears?
I care not sweetest lips though lies ye tell!
I will not know! I do not dare to prove,
　　　　If Sleep mock Love!

A SONG OF SPRING.

THE thrush has a pean to sing,
  The lilacs are bending to hear,
'Tis the same old, old message of Spring,
  They find it still new, still dear,
So the thrush is contented to sing
  And the lilacs are bending to hear.

Tinted eggs are the pride of the nest,
  Tinted blossoms the pride of the tree,
But the pride of the heart unconfess't
  In silence still hidden must be;
While the thrush sings of hope in the nest
  And the lilacs boast joy on the tree.

O! Love has a pean to sing,
  But who is there list'ning to hear?
While the day dreaming, deepen in Spring,
  And Spring fades away in the year.
O! Love, be contented to sing,
  For some hidden violet may hear!

A BALLAD OF APRIL.

DARK April clouds, O pass away!
  What mischief are ye brewing?
Across the sky dark shades ye lay
  Which will be love's undoing;
With skies so sullen, cold and grey,
  What lover would go wooing.

O! April sun, why glory hide,
  As if afraid of shining?
When golden robes with joyful pride
  For love you should be lining,
And wreaths 'of flowers, in love-knots tied,
  The sunbeams should be twining.

VARIANT.

Sweet April clouds! Pass ye or stay,
  No harm ye can be brewing
Since love heeds not the shades ye lay,
  Nor recks what suns are doing;
If skies be blue or sullen grey
  My lover yet comes wooing!

SOMETIMES.

SOMETIMES by a sunbeam's sudden shimmer,
   Sometimes in the shadow of a cloud,
Sometimes 'mid the twilight's tender glimmer,
   I have seen Love pale and proud.
Sometimes tears upon his lashes,
   Sometimes grief within his breast;
Sometimes smile on smile outflashes—
   Who shall say which mood is best?

Sometimes songs of rapture singing,
   Sometimes silent, slow of breath;
Sometimes thro' heav'n's azure winging,
   Sometimes weary unto death;
Sometimes waking, sometimes dreaming,
   But at all times most divine,
For Love's face thro' all this seeming,
   Is the same Belov'd as thine!

AN OCEAN FANCY.

Out of the coral caves under the sea,
The mermaids peeped half dreamily,
Dazzled awhile by the moon, whose sighs
Had shaken their souls, and opened their eyes,
   And by her gleams
   Destroyed their dreams;
Under the waves, in the coral caves,
 The mermaids woke and sang to me
   A sweet and thrilling melody!

"O! mortal eyes, where sorrow lies,
Because the world is full of pain,
We know your tears are harbingers
Of Love, and so are never vain;
 But we are here such grief to cheer
 So fling away that humid veil,
   Arise! Arise!
   Upon the skies

The moon has drawn a silver trail,
　　　　And we must guide
　　　　The flowing tide
Which swoons beneath that vision pale!

"Come see our bow'rs, the ocean flow'rs
Have woven charms to bind the hours,
There thou shalt sleep, and we will keep
A watch against all evil pow'rs;
Or would'st thou wake, the air shall break
Into a thousand melodies,
While mem'ries meet of all things sweet
Soothed by delicious harmonies."

Ah! my soul was enthralled by a charm so vast,
I felt heav'n had dawned over earth at last
I cared not for life, I cared not for death,
While that tender song yearned to me so from
　　　beneath.
　　　　　What mattered the fold
　　　　　Of the water's cold?

Were they not bearing my soul afar
        To that pearl-paved deep
        Where the breezes sleep
And the weary and wounded wavelets are ?

"Away! away! O'er the starlit bay
Our clinging, shadowy bodies sway ;
Dost feel the bliss of the ocean's kiss,
As its glittering foam-drops round thee play ?
List, oh list! for athwart the mist
The moon has bound on the night's dark brow,
Strange spirits sing of many a thing
Whereof thou could'st not know till now."

So we passed by Horizon's mystical gate,
Which none may pass till unbarr'd by fate,
In the darkling depths it looked dark and grim
But I found it was only the silver rim
Of a halo that shines 'twixt heaven and earth
To proclaim when a royal wave has birth.
   And there the kisses garnered lie
   That pass between the sea and sky,

c

Whereby the 'witching moon doth make
Her charms to keep the stars awake.
> They bore me thence
> To the low cadence
The amorous waters chanted low
Of a passion no human heart may know.

Then we threaded a labyrinthian way
'Twixt sands that in golden masses lay,
Till we came to the realms of the drownèd Dead
'Neath a network of seaweed canopied;
> O! never a sound
> Broke their rest profound,
But trembling bubbles light and soft
On wings of azure soar aloft
To fetch fair dreams from Paradise
For those pale Dreamers' closèd eyes
O! there they rest contentedly
Beneath the bosom of the sea,
While tempests rage and great ships ride
Above them on the swelling tide
Serenely calm and satisfied!

" Come follow, follow, such thoughts are hollow,

While winds abound the waves must swallow

Human hearts and human gains,

Leave thou them and their remains.

But a scene of revelry in our bow'rs thou shalt

 see,

 There are poets and their fancies

 Brightening all things with their glances,

   Lovers' whispers there have breath

   Tho' love's lips are cold in death.

We will teach thee subtle charms

Woven 'mid the storm's alarms

Whereby power of all have we

'Neath the bosom of the sea!

" Lo! within a crystal casket

Lies thy heart's desire—ask it,

Ope thy treasure and unmask it,

 Till adown the veilèd spheres

 Visions dawn of future years ;

Thou shalt learn bewitchingly

As ourselves to sing and sigh ;

Also every subtle use
Of the wave's prismatic hues.
   O! the swaying of the flowers,
   O! the rapture of the hours
   Spent within our happy bowers!"

But the morning dawns o'er the smiling bay,
And kisses its tender dreams away,
Yes, kisses the same unconscious lips
Which the moon has pressed; see, she pallid slips,
A lovelorn thing, 'neath a pitying cloud.
        O! trust not thou
        To a mermaid's vow,
They mock thee with rippling laughter loud!
        They have no bow'rs,
        Their vaunted pow'rs
        Vanish before these sunbeam showers.
Yet, who shall say that Ocean mirth
Is falser than the joy of earth?

IT WAS YOUR NAME!

RONDEL.

It was your name which, when song's pinions tired,
Refreshed their drooping weariness and fired
With sweet new strength their weakness, till in
    flame
Up leapt the passionate utterance love desired,
And hope once more in tender semblance came,
        It was your name!

It was your name that made me understand
The yearning message the sea flings the sand,
And the soft blush that decks the rose with shame
When suddenly the sunshine clasps the land;
And why with the moon's kiss the clouds grow
    tame—
        It was your name!

The glacier's icy heart doth proudly flow
In happy tears since the sun will it so

So for a sweeter reason, yet the same,

My soul's desire set free doth heavenward go,

Till love's blest lips in tender tones proclaim,

It was your name!

A FRAGMENT.

I WEEP a happy shower of tears
    Because love overflows my soul;
A rainbow circles heav'n's spheres
    And crowns its sweetest goal!

Diviner than the royal hue
    Which wraps the dawn in orient skies,
This sombre tinted cloud, this dew
    Of love that dims my eyes.

More eloquent than words, no song
    Of mine shall dare to thrill love's lute,
Weeping for joy, heav'n's heights among,
    I marvel and am mute!

MORNING AND NIGHT.

A COMPARISON.

THE sweet day rose in beauty so serene
  I laid upon its wings my heart's desire ;
No shade of doubt could hover in between,
  It seemed an altar lit with sacred fire,
      A song upon a lyre !

The sad day set, a red glow 'mid deep gloom,
  I laid on its bruised wings my heart's despair;
And all the west was awful as a tomb,
  An altar, desecrated, lonely, bare,
      A wild unanswered prayer !

IF LOVE BE LIKE A ROSE.

If love be like a rose in beauty's pride,
If the sweet fragrance of a rose can be
Compared to the desire love's pinions hide,
Lest eyes profane should mock that mystery,
Then tell me where love's faded petal goes
If truly she be likened to a rose?

The withered rose leaves all unheeded lie,
Made foul with mould, upon the earth's cold breast,
Till the wind whirls them as he passes by,
Treating their bygone splendour as a jest;
Somewhere perchance a wind as idly blows
Forgotten loves which once bloomed like a rose?

Just as they are, however stained with grief,
With scarce a trace to mark they once were fair;
Just as it is, find me one pain-scared leaf,
Within my heart a tomb lies ready, there
It shall obtain the long deserved repose;
Find me one petal of love's faded rose!

I should not fear the royal hue grown pale,
I should not miss the perfume long since shed,
When first its tender heart began to fail,
A thousand-fold more precious now 'tis dead,
Around it still some glory clings, who knows
It may be sweeter than the fair, false rose!

Ah, no! the heart knows better, and must speak,
It is the nature of the rose to die,
And so we prove the simile most weak
For love should live for ever, that is why,
Altho' the world be searched, no garden close
Guards love's dead sweet, tho' fragile as a rose!

TRIOLET.

A song of hope loud sings the wind
    Adown the skies fast flying—
"Spring's golden tresses I unbind!"
A song of hope loud sings the wind
While breezes whisper soft behind,
    "Cold winter is a-dying!"
A song of hope loud sings the wind,
    Adown the skies fast flying!

SONNETS.

DESIRE UNATTAINED.

I.

Is love all powerful? ah! then in sighs
Why dost thou, heart, these precious hours spend?
Why must the day in gloomy darkness end,
And leave thee still out-barr'd from Paradise?
No answering words to thy entreaties rise,
And the sad echo, tho' it seem a friend,
Is powerless one wild regret to mend;
Thou can'st not conjure up those absent eyes!
Nay, love is weak, or thou had'st had thy fill
Of sure delight, which art with love so stored,
And one low prayer had given thee back again
That fair desire, which all prayers ask in vain;
Oh! love is weak, his pinions never soared,
Since fate he fears, and hope he cannot kill!

II.

What is there in the universe above
That can compare with this my love for thee?
Not the stars' yearning eyes, which draw the sea,
As on its heaving breast their shadows rove;
Nor yet the mighty winds, which only move
When some strange impulse prompts them to fly
    free—
But ever yearning, strong perpetually
Is the absorbing greatness of my love!
And what then in the sorrowing earth beneath
Is liken to it? The volcanic fire
That rends a mountain's beauteous crest in twain?
Or some slight flow'r that seeks the sun in vain?
Look! and in both, oh! Heart of my desire,
Thou shalt find something of love's trembling
    breath!

III.

Like some seabird that pauses in mid-flight
Among the waves and far off spies the shore

Swelling a beauteous landscape bathed in light,
And longs for peace, a want unknown before,
Growing weary of the waters' restless might,
The seething foam and everlasting roar;
Even his boundless freedom at that sight
Becomes a bond, since there he may not soar.
So, faint with yearning, have I far off seen
The fair sweet line of my desire lie
Beyond the utmost limit of my love,
With all the world's unquiet ways between,—
And wept to know, howe'er my soul's wings fly,
Yet in that blessèd land they cannot rove !

TO A NIGHTINGALE.

O! NIGHTINGALE, that singest out of sight,
On some scent-laden bush, thy heart's desire,
Till the dark bosom of the list'ning night
Swells with the kindling of a passionate fire,
Reveal to me if love should weep or sing,
If like yon rose, my heart may yet unveil
The sweet that lies, a lovely hidden thing,
Within my breast, like hers in petals pale?
I may not soar like thee thro' midnight skies,
I dare not whisper even to a breeze
The glory of my hope, lest it prove shame—
Ah! ere the morning spread her wings of flame,
Give me some token, love's sad doubt to ease,
Sing me some message 'mong those melodies!

A LONELY POPPY.

THERE was a lonely poppy, hidden deep
Among the golden spears of ripening corn,
An outcast from their love, since lowlier born;
While the glad earth a carnival did keep
She blood-red petals shed, her tears, so weep
The sorrowing flow'rs; then patiently, forlorn
Waited in eager grief for each new morn
Till harvest time should bring some hand to reap.
Oh, foolish poppy! Had'st thou raised awhile
Thy drooping head, rich blessing had'st thou known;
Since slantwise, thro' the swaying of the wheat,
The moon gazed at thee oft, with pitying smile;
And tenderly the dew's lips sought thy own
Finding thy lonely beauty very sweet!

A THUNDERSTORM; OR, SATAN'S FALL.

ADOWN Infinity God's sentence rolled,
Dooming for ever Lucifer the proud,
Till all creation heard it uttered loud,
And planet unto planet echoing told.
Then from the wond'rous depths and manifold
Which wrapt God's throne, the bright Shekinah cloud,
With serpent gleaming eyes and head low bowed,
The Prince of Darkness fell, like liquid gold.
And as the splendour of a lightning flash,
Losing itself amid the yawning night,
Is followed by the thunder's mighty crash,
So to unfathomed depths from that pure height
He disappeared; when a triumphant cry
Burst like the thunder, down Infinity!

D

THY LOVE AND MINE.

THY love and mine, what are they like? even this,
To cold clear moonlight, beautiful and grand,
That sees the restless waves leap up to kiss
The silent, shadowy outline of the sand;
Such is thy love, a radiance great and sweet
Wrapping my heart, which yet must fret beneath,
Because I may not know how thine doth beat,
I cannot feel if passion sway thy breath.

Come closer, my Belov'd, who art so far,
I can no longer bear fate's cruel test;
Let some convulsion blend the moon and star,
That pulse with pulse may meet, and be at rest.
Then kiss me, till I die upon thy breast:
Thy love and mine, how different they are!

THE ELM TREE AND POOL.

THERE is a meadow where an elm tree grows
Shadowing a pool, so close beneath she lies
The lightest breeze that thro' his branches sighs,
Ruffling the glossy leaves, reflected shows
In those clear depths, where love's own shades
    repose.
And sometimes glimpses of the summer skies
The jealous boughs let thro', then her dark eyes
Flash azure, while the glimmering emerald glows.
Ah! tender pool, most surely it is well
To mirror pleasant truths, but what shall chance
When all that grace is shorn by winter's breath?
Wilt thou have courage still the truth to tell?
Darest thou answer love's inquiring glance
With fearless gaze, where passion swoons in death?

REJECTED.

THE weird wild beauty of a highland glen
A passionate mountain torrent breaks apart,
Seeming to mock Love's patient, broken heart,
A parallel 'tween nature and 'tween men.
Scattered around great heaps of silent stone,
Whereon the stains of many a cycle lie,
Unheeding purple hills and thou and I,
And Love, whose presence thou perceived alone.
Who would not weep, rememb'ring, bitter tears
For so much solitude and sorrowing sweet?
My haunted heart that rushing torrent hears,
And echoes it with ev'ry restless beat;
But Love, whose glory circumvents the years,
Perchance this grief shall make his crown complete?

MONOTONY.

EACH day with swelling heart, O! mighty sea,
Thou clingest to the shore, then with one stride
Leavest her lonely in thy ebbing tide.
Does she not tire of thy inconstancy?
Each night, pale moon, adown Infinity
Thou glidest like a fair and mournful bride,
Bereft of hope, with only love to guide.
Art not thou heartsick with monotony?

We who lose something of our life each hour,
And know not what each dawning day may bring,
Yet languish at this strong resistless pow'r,
Waiting and yearning for some newer thing,
We know so well that winter kills the flow'r
Which summer cherished as the child of spring!

THE LEGEND OF THE OLIVE TREES.

O! TENDER, quivering Olive, was it fear
That blanched thy emerald colour softly green
And shed instead this silver pallid sheen,
Or sorrow, for the stricken Godhead near?
The legend runneth,—in the moonlight clear,
On that dread night of agony divine,
Grief overcame that saddened heart of thine,
Till in the silence fell a glittering tear!
Then wept the stars, with all their million eyes,
Then trembled the hard earth, while the wind's
    breath
Went moaning with the bitterness of death,
And all the angels sighed in Paradise;
Yet stars shine bright, and earth is calm, but *thou*
Showest thy grief in steadfast pallor *now!*

WHAT'S IN A NAME?

WHAT's in a name?   Just this, that when I hear
Thine spoken Love wildly my heart doth beat
Because our very spirits seem to meet
Within the mem'ries which do then appear.
As if to wipe away all foolish fear,
A moonbeam did a tender flower greet,
Nestling itself among the perfume sweet,
Soothing the dewy sorrow lying there.

A gentle breeze, that fanneth into flame
A fire that burns concealed; a rosy wreath
Which crowns the yearning brow of poesy,
A reason for my heart's humanity,
A love that lives without a fear of death,
All this, Belov'd, I find within thy name!

LOVE'S PLAY.

ANACREONTIC.

LOVE came to me one summer's day
And prick'd me with his dart in play,
Two rose leaves on my eyes he laid,
Bewild'ring them with scented shade,
    While silently a chain he wove
    About my soul, the Tyrant, Love!

But I was happy as his slave
Such royal gifts to me he gave;
By day a gold bowl of delight,
And ah! such glorious dreams by night.
    Heav'n seemed around me, not above—
    He stole my soul, the Charmer, Love!

And it was still a summer's day
When he grew weary of his play,
So took the rose leaves from my eyes,
Revealing then a world of sighs;
    And left my wounded heart to prove—
    How cruel is the Deceiver, Love!

A SIGH!

Ah! happy moon! to so serenely gaze
Whene'er thou wilt upon thy love the earth,
For thou can'st dream away the summer days
In yon blue vault, till silent night gave birth
To that sweet dark which marks for thee love's
    ways.

Scarce wonder then that thou can'st be so calm,
So sure of love, so beautiful and pale,
The midnight breezes weave for thee a charm
Whose subtle power was never known to fail,
While starry shadows soothe all vague alarm.

Yet could I, like thee, know, my yearning eyes
Should surely see each eve my heart's desire,
More eagerly I'd seek to climb the skies,
More passionately the stars should swing their fire!
But thou art patient, peaceful, strangely wise!

The soft wing'd nights glide swiftly into days,
And many a time thy dreaming eyes awake
To smile on realised hopes; when shall mine gaze
On that dear face for which they saddening ache?
Ah! pitying moon, prepare for love those ways!

THE OTHER SIDE OF HEAVEN.

BEYOND the sun's light shedding eyes,
Or shade of myriad lesser spheres,
The other side of Heaven lies,
Unruled by fate, undimmed by tears.

My fancy bade me enter there,
My love lent wings, and speed my grief,
My scorn a warning gave, "Beware!
Of dreams which promise such relief."

Across an azure sea of space
Whose waves seemed clouds of jewelled foam
I passed, where panting vapours trace
The starry pathway to their home.

Short-sighted race of struggling men
Whose life and love seem slaves to fate,
How vast, how free is Heaven when
Contrasted with your little state!

Such majesty of silence clasps
Those dim recesses of the sky,
No lightning flares, no thunder gasps,
No roaring tempests climb as high.

Yet each soul yearns for its own heaven,
Each builds, is its own architect,
And death the puny plans has given
To God, to sanction or reject.

I would believe we may attain
Our ideals, marvellously wrought
And changed, made perfect art, where pain
Withdraws its cruel hold on thought.

I must believe the seeds of love
Which flourish 'mid disease and death,
Whose presence these our bodies prove
With every breath, the heart is worth;

I must believe no grain is lost,
That each will grow a perfect flow'r;

O! guard it well, despise the cost,
Though Time and Fate unite their pow'r!

The other side of Heaven?   Let be
These faithless fears; my heart's Belov'd
I turn from selfish peace to thee
And rove the earth, where thou hast roved!

RONDELS.

'TWAS NOT IN VAIN!

'Twas not in vain ye bloomed, ungathered rose,
Though no fond eye thy tender beauty knows,
Nor eager lips those fragrant leaves caress;
Have the winds failed to woo and love thee less?
Nay, wafted on the air thy sweets have lain,
　　　　　　　'Twas not in vain!

Nothing is useless here, however slight,
A slender dewdrop on a mountain's height
That glistens but a moment in the sun,
Crownèd in gold, some secret good hath done,
Unknown may be, but to the earth's breast gain,
　　　　　　　'Twas not in vain!

'Twas not in vain we loved, tho' many tears
Have dimmed our yearning eyes, tho' many years
Have drifted cruelly down Time's vast sea
And striven to drown that one sweet memory;
Live it once more, and say with passionate pain
　　　　　　　'Twas not in vain!

GOOD-BYE, A LONG GOOD-BYE!

GOOD-BYE, a long good-bye to love,
And all love's dreams which facts disprove,
Silence the lyre once his, let be
That fair false form of minstrelsy,
Till on the air the echoes die,
   Good-bye, a long good-bye!

O! mountains steep, which once seemed rough
To part love's ways, scarce wide enough
I fear the world is for love's pain,—
We find the same sweet path again
Where once we sang, where now we sigh,
   Good-bye, a long good-bye!

Good-bye, a long good-bye to fears
Now realised by these sad tears,
Good-bye, belovèd lips, still sweet
To me in spite of fate's deceit;
Mine sigh in silent agony,
   Good-bye, a long good-bye!

LOVE STOOPED AND SAID.

LOVE stooped and said to yon complaining rose
Some sweet low word, for see her trouble goes
Fading in perfumed sighs upon the air,
Swaying a sunbeam's wings that rested there;
What was the charm, making her blush so red,
        Love stooped and said?

Restless with grief, my heart breathed forth a song
Which far away the mocking echoes flung;
But one in pity heard that trembling strain,
Those passionate notes were not sent forth in vain;
A word that made grief's chant joy's psalm instead—
        Love stooped and said!

Than all the summer's store more wealth, oh! rose,
Have we, since that divinest secret grows

More beauteous in our hearts than all things fair;
Sweet, like the hope fulfilled crowning a prayer,
That subtle word, leaving us comforted—

              Love stooped and said!

DELAY NOT SWEET!

Delay not Sweet, the wide world's breadth apart,
Twice has the crescent moon become a sphere,
And autumn's lips are kissing dead the year
Which, smiling, swoons contented, but my heart
Sighs ev'ry time its passionate pulses beat—
           Delay not Sweet!

What use the sunlight shimmering on the sea,
Or lang'rous lily perfumes lightly borne
Upon a zephyr's wings? When thus forlorn
The joys of nature bring no joy to me
Each hastening hour I pray to fly more fleet—
           Delay not Sweet!

Delay not Sweet, for troubles come apace,
Each day some tint of life's fair rose expires,
And doubt destroys the dream that love desires;
Ah! cleave these cruel leagues of sterile space
Where pitying echoes murmur as they meet—
           Delay not Sweet!

THE FLIGHT OF THE MUSE.

FAR off and far away my fair Muse flies,
She will not linger, tho' I whisper "Stay!"
Leaving behind her roseate, radiant skies,
Bright with Love's dawn of possibilities;
High heavens I may not reach bereft of wings,
Great joys I cannot hymn without her aid,
   She flies far off, away!
For the Nine Maidens will not brook these things,
To worship other idols near their shrines,
But ah! I lingered by Love's altar close,
And swooned amid the perfumed incense there,
I prayed to Love, a fervent, yearning prayer,
And at the dawning of the new sweet day—
   My Muse flew far away!
Thus silent, soul entranced, I watching see
Sweet dreams unfurled, which like clouds dew be-
  pearled
Flash whiter than the young moon's purity,
When first it meets the love gaze of the world;

Silent, with lips and voice that cannot bear
The burthen of such passionate delight;
Yet happier than all stars within the sky,
Swelling with song the spheres would weep to hear,
This heart of mine, from which my Muse took
    flight
Because, Belov'd, thy Love's wings hovered near!
Come closer, then, until I see no sight
Beyond their all embracing tender shade,
Upon their strength my weakness let me lay;
Then, thro' the boundless blue of Heaven's arcade
        Let us fly far away!

WHEN THOU ART GONE!

WHEN thou art gone, "what shall I do?"
When thou art gone, I shall not be;
These eyes, these lips that love you so
May seem still to be part of me,
My *heart* will be as dead as stone
      When thou art gone!
What could I do? Live in the past,
Show to the mocking world my pain?
Proving how much to me thou wast,
Revealing love can be in vain;
Howe'er I grieve, I grieve alone
      When thou art gone.
When thou art gone! there rings love's knell,
There breathes the last sigh of my heart
In one wild pitiful farewell—
It cleaves pale passionate lips apart.
"What will love do?" Love is undone—
      When thou art gone!

ODE TO MEMORY.

LIKE balmy ripples of an azure tide
   That smile all day around a far-off shore,
And nearer, ever nearer, fain would glide,
   But still remain as distant as before,
Sweet Mem'ry seems, when wafted on her wings
Some mystic odour of the past she brings.

Or like a wandering star that sails unloosed
   From the safe anchorage of peaceful heav'n
To kiss earth's throbbing breast, where love is used
   With thankful eyes to watch the deep'ning even;
O! meteor flashing through divinest tears!
O! glory hallowing the pale, dead years!

And is there then no mem'ry in the tomb?
   No polished mirror where the poor Dead see
Amid that drear, predominating gloom
   The radiant vision of what used to be?
A vision purified from sin and pain,
Proving not all their feverish life was vain.

Ah! if there be none such, pale, peaceful Dead
   I do not envy you your awful calm;
Better to live with ghosts of glories fled,
   Better to breathe in restless vague alarm
Than lie unmated in so dull a rest—
Without one secret yearning in the breast.

Like balmy ripples of an azure tide,
   Around my soul for ever sweetly lave
Divinest Memory! Nor let time's chasm wide
   Prevent the charm of thy delicious wave;
Still shine a guiding star thro' sorrow's night,
Gilding the faded past with magic light!

TRIOLET.

I HAVE seen love's eyes to-day,
  So my heart be satisfied;
Faithless doubts, O pass away!
I have seen love's eyes to-day,
Every pulse has felt the sway
  Of a passion glorified!
I have seen love's eyes to-day,
  So my heart be satisfied!

IF ALL BE WELL.

If all be well, and fate at last hath blest
My yearning life with your sweet love, then lest
Some wand'ring echo of the world should break
My soul's content, be silent for love's sake:
So let heav'n fling a challenge unto hell—
　　　If all be well!

Since beauty seems more beautiful when lit
By some soft light that half o'ershadows it,
As in the inmost heart of the great sea
No ripple moves, no lightest breeze can be;
So let love by a passionate silence tell—
　　　If all be well!

CUPID'S CASKET.

AH! what have you in your casket, little Cupid,
   Little Cupid brought for me,
That your azure pinions quiver
With the weight thereof, sweet giver
Of hid treasure, dare I ask it
   In love's sacred name to see?

"In my casket I have lying
   For the roses' hearts more scent,
And a new song for the linnet,
That is all, I think, that's in it
Save a mortal's heart, whose sighing
   Seems a breeze of discontent.

" All the song and scent's bespoken,
   Will the sighing do as well?"

Oh have pity, little Cupid!
Are you cruel, or but stupid,
For love asks no sweeter token
　　Than that sighing heart doth tell!

ON BEING ASKED TO WRITE AN ODE
TO THE DAWN.

Unto the dawn an ode to write
　　Perchance an easy task 'twould be,
But to the Dawn that woke that night,
　　Unveiled love's dreaming eyes to see,
　　　　Ask not of me!

Ah Sweet! the boldest nightingale
　　Could scarce attempt to sing that strain;
His passionate heart would panting fail
　　Ere love's high keynote he could gain,
　　　　Where joy clasps pain.

Beyond the heav'n, where stars are born,
　　My song's slight wings would have to fly
Ere I could hymn that perfect Dawn.
　　Love's lips are dumb with ecstasy,
　　　　And so am I!

HOW IS LOVE BLEST?

Love, with a wound at heart,
Love, by a fear opprest,
Love, a world's breadth apart,
    How is Love blest?
Love, with her lips struck dumb,
Love, made by Fate a jest,
Weeping, unkissed, grief-numb,
    How is Love blest?

By that same wound intense,
Salved by a mem'ry sweet,
By the world's vapour dense,
    Severing to meet;
By those same lips whose song
Thrills where no discords beat,
Heav'n's highest strains among,
    Love doth compete!

Love, by a cross recrowned,
Love, by a doubt truth guess't,
Love, by a world disowned,
　　Built her own nest;
Love, with lips pure to kiss,
Flings back to death, Fate's jest;
Love is divine—by this
　　Love makes Love blest!

A GOOD-BYE.

HALF the world dies in this good-bye; then wait
One moment more while I take tearful leave
Of all old treasures garnered in by fate,
Of sad sweet roses scattered in our way
And clinging tendrils of that vine which weave
A halo round the grapes we crush to-day!

Half only dies, would that the whole world gasped
Its soul out thro' my breath; but thou hast left
A remnant yet within my cold hands clasped,
A kiss upon my lips still rests congealed;
'Twere better far to be of all bereft
With sightless eyes forgetfulness had sealed!

Crimson, the glory of departing day,
Crimson, the sweetness in red poppies slain,
Crimson, the warrior's gory-tracked way;
Why then should thou and I be yet so pale
While 'neath our breasts lies bleeding fast the stain
Crimson with grief and shame of loves that fail!

We cannot tell, "good-bye" is ever decked
With pallor, that love only understands;
The too frail frigate of delight lies wrecked
By boisterous winds which life's destruction weave.
The moment Sweet is o'er, on fate's dark sands
Pass by, while I amid the wreckage grieve!

RONDEL IN MONO-RHYME.

COULD I believe, could I believe
The soul's high hopes did not deceive
Some long-yearned good I might achieve,
    Could I believe!

Could I believe, could I believe
That sorrow might past wrong retrieve,
Then sighs of grief my breast should heave,
    Could I believe!

Could I believe, could I believe
Desire, reward may yet receive,
What tender visions faith should weave,
    Could I believe!

Could I believe, could I believe
Thy love were mine, death might bereave,
Grant passion but one short reprieve,
I should not fear, I should not grieve,
    Could I believe!

F

LOVE'S HEIGHT.

Oh let us rest here! We have climbed enough
Beyond the world into this love-girt land,
There far below in atmospheric mist
Lie the great mountains, rugged, steep, and rough,
And there the sun illumines with a band
Of flame the happy height where first we kissed.

Wilt thou not rest here? To go higher still
I dare not, we should touch yon pale-faced moon;
The glistening stars would fright me with their
      gaze,
The breeze that flieth past them is too chill;
See, even now the ether makes me swoon,
And thou art drifting from me 'mid the haze!

Rest here for ever, this alone is sweet
To be together, fold me to thy breast,
Perchance God looking down Eternity
Will suffer us to lie here 'neath His feet,

Will see our joy, and pitying say "'Tis best,
Love is the heaven of humanity!"

Yet no, we may not stay, we must return
With night's deep shadows to the earth again ;
I will not risk to disillusion all
By a false flight ; the eagle does not spurn
The lowly valley—'tis the lesser pain
To leave heav'n guiltless than to sin and fall.

One more embrace, merge all thy tenderness
Within thy lips, mirror me in thy eyes ;
Ah ! how this vapour blinds me from thy sight ;
My heart beats faintly for great bitterness.
Dear ! 'tis enough, tho' knowing Paradise,
We could not breathe on Love's sublimest height !

LOVE'S WAY IS BEST!

RONDEL.

LOVE'S way is best, tho' we find him sleeping
With a rose for his pillow, his lyre unstrung.
Chide him not, lest suddenly swift upleaping
He trample the rose, leave his songs unsung;
Though Faith find patience an irksome test,
  Love's way is best!

Far o'er the hills, where the mist is wreathing
A silver shroud for the dying day,
He may frightened fly, should he hear us breathing
One sigh too deep for this long delay.
Though the shadows deepen toward the west,
  Love's way is best!

Love's way is best, tho' he never waken,
Leave the dream divine 'neath those veilèd eyes;
Tho' the heart rebel, as a thing forsaken,
Tho' we cannot grasp such mysteries,
Oh, yearning soul! oh, passionate breast!
  Love's way is best!

REVERIE ON A DEAD YEAR.

THERE came last night a sound of symphonies,
Borne on the frail wings of an infant wind,
The voices of the dead Year's memories.

My heart had built a bridge toward my mind,
A tender structure whereon these might rest;
And roses round their brows were yet entwined.

As gently sink the sunbeams in the west
On some midsummer's eve, most loth to sleep
Since the earth's fragrance on their lips has prest

A kiss whose strength can climb ev'n heav'n's
       steep;—
So, ling'ringly, those subtle strains did move
Around my soul O mystery more deep

Than flaming planets in the skies above!
Make yet divine these happy human tears,
A heart's pure offering, at thy shrine, O Love!

No summer ever smiled in other years,
No winter yet was crowned with snow so pure
As these, whose glory shall not disappear,

But beyond Time and Fate they shall endure,
Immortal memories, heed no year's death!
Sing still your peans, comfort, reassure

The faltering echoes of Love's passionate breath,
Till, drenched with beauty, the new year doth wake
To greet not earth, but heav'n, above, beneath!

LOVE HEEDS NOT TIME!

RONDEL.

"LOVE heeds not time," the foolish rose breathed
    low
When ere her season she began to blow,
Woo'd by the amorous breezes of the Spring,
Beguiled by the glad look of everything,
The gold-bell'd crocus mocked with echoing chime,
        "Love heeds not time!"

Ah! eager rose, far better 'twere to wait,
E'en though the Summer make her coming late;
'Tis true the first kiss of the sun you get,
The pearliest drops of dew your petals wet,
But soon that dew shall weep, congealed with rime,
        "Love heeds not time!"

There is no pity for her, no redress;
The cruel frost wrecks all that loveliness!

So, sun forsaken, and betrayed she dies,
With crystal sorrow frozen in her eyes;
Yet faithful gasps, with her last breath sublime,
" Love heeds not time ! "

LONDON : DIGBY, LONG & Co., PUBLISHERS,
18 Bouverie Street, Fleet Street, E.C.

18 Bouverie Street,
Fleet Street,
London, E.C.

THE NEWCASTLE DAILY CHRONICLE (the great Newspaper of the North), in speaking of good and wholesome fiction, refers to the "*high reputation that Messrs DIGBY, LONG & CO. enjoy for the publication of first-class novels.*"

A Selection from the List of Books

PUBLISHED BY

Messrs DIGBY, LONG & CO.

LIST OF BOOKS.

A Modern Milkmaid. By the Author of "Commonplace Sinners." In 3 vols., crown 8vo, cloth extra, 31s. 6d. Cheap Edition in Railway Picture Boards, 2s.

" . . . the book is remarkable and powerful, and it certainly ought to be read, and read attentively."—*National Observer*.

" A book which gives evidence of much literary power. . . . The novel is one which commands attention. The author has the literary faculty sufficiently developed to enable him or her to join the front rank of writers of fiction."—*Pictorial World*.

Wildwater Terrace. By REGINALD E. SALWEY. In 2 vols., crown 8vo, cloth extra, 21s.

" We strongly advise novel-readers to make the acquaintance of ' Wildwater Terrace.' An eminently readable and interesting book."—*Court Circular*.

" A powerful story, with some peculiarly dramatic situations and a good deal of descriptive skill."—*Literary World*.

" Mr Salwey weaves a terrible piece of mystery, and the reader who follows it in the making will certainly get a great deal of entertainment out of it."—*Athenæum*.

John Bolt, Indian Civil Servant; A Tale of Old Haileybury and India. By R. W. LODWICK, late Bombay Civil Service. In 2 vols., crown 8vo, cloth extra, 21s.

"Mr Lodwick's simple and graphic manner. . . . The author's lively sketches of what may now be called the old Overland Route, and the dramatic incidents of the Mutiny are all excellent in their way, but the book has greater merit of possessing a deep human interest that never loses its hold on the reader's imagination."—*Morning Post*.

The Heiress of Beechfield. By M. E. BALDWIN. In 2 vols. Cloth extra, price 21s.   [*Just Published*.

Hamtura. A Tale of an unknown Land. Second Edition. By H. S. LOCKHART-ROSS. In handsome binding, gilt lettered and bevelled boards, price 6s. Postage, 4½d.

" A work of considerable promise. . . . His descriptions of the island and people of Hamtura are excellent. . . . The idea of the Raven is excellent, almost epic ; and the scenes in the temple of Hamtura are very impressively done. The book is distinctly promising."—*Saturday Review*.

Beneath Your Very Boots. Second Edition. By C. J. HYNE, Author of "A Matrimonial Mixture." Crown 8vo, cloth extra, price 6s. Postage, 4½d.

" By no means miss reading ' Beneath Your Very Boots.' The story is absolutely new, and cleverly worked out."—*Athenæum*.

The Belvidere. By WILLIAM DWARRIS. Crown 8vo, cloth extra, price 6s. Postage, 4½d.

"A well written and really powerful story."—*Newcastle Daily Chronicle.*

Paul Creighton. By GERTRUDE CARR DAVISON. Crown 8vo, cloth extra, price 6s. Postage, 4½d.

" A first-class novel, for besides affording the reader much pleasurable excitement, it gives him something to think of that is elevating. The scenes are lifelike, and the sweet character of the heroine leaves nothing to be desired. The author has succeeded in placing before the public a very good work, and one that should be read, therefore."—*Hereford Times.*

Leslie. By the Author of " A Modern Milkmaid," etc., etc. In handsome pictorial binding, gilt lettered. Crown 8vo, price 6s. Postage, 4½d.

Leading Women of the Restoration. Lady Russell, Lady Warwick, Lady Maynard, Mrs Hutchinson, Mrs Godolphin. With portraits. Dedicated to Lord Arthur Russell. By Mrs GRACE JOHNSTONE. Demy 8vo, cloth extra, price 6s. Postage, 6d. [*Just Published.*]

A Ride Across Iceland in the Summer of 1891. By the Rev. W. T. McCORMICK, F.R.G.S., F.S.A., etc. With frontispiece. Crown 8vo, cloth extra, price 2s. 6d. Postage, 3d. [*Just Published.*]

The Jolly Roger. A Tale of Sea Heroes and Pirates. By HUME NISBET, Author of " Bail Up," " A Colonial Tramp," "The Land of the Hibiscus Blossom," "The Savage Queen," " Eight Bells," etc., etc. In handsome pictorial binding, with frontispiece and vignette title page by the Author. Crown 8vo, price 3s. 6d. Postage, 4½d. [*Just Published.*]

Won by Honour. A Novel. By VANDA. Crown 8vo, cloth extra, price 6s. Postage 4½d.

" A novel of considerable promise . . . the writing is forcible and to the point."—*People.*

" A pleasing story. The volume may be read with pleasure."—*Scotsman.*

Phil : A Story of School Life. By ALFRED HARPER. Crown 8vo, cloth extra, price 3s. 6d. Postage, 3d.

" A bright and interesting sketch . . . it may be read with much pleasure for its evident honesty of purpose and truth to nature."—*Daily Chronicle.*

" Not only boys, but also grown-up people will enjoy this fresh, wholesome story of school life . . . the book deserves to reach a second edition."—*Vanity Fair.*

18 Bouverie Street, Fleet Street, London, E.C.

Chronology and Analysis of International Law. By WILLIAM PERCY PAIN, LL.B. (University of London), of the Inner Temple, Barrister-at-Law. (First Class Studentship of the Inns of Court for Jurisprudence and International Law, Hilary Term (1880). Crown 8vo, cloth extra, price 3s. 6d. Postage, 3d.

"Should be of considerable use to the student of international law."—*Low Times.*

"A valuable handbook for the student of international law. The arrangement of the book is admirable. Students will find it in all respects a most admirable help to the study of the great subjects to which it relates."—*Scotsman.*

Ruy Blas. Translated from the French of Victor Hugo. By W. D. S. ALEXANDER, Author of "The Lonely Guiding Star." Crown 8vo, cloth extra, bevelled boards, price 3s. 6d. Postage, 3d.

"A really fine English version. Mr Alexander's is, we think, the best translation that has yet been done."—*Pictorial World.*

"The task of rendering this fine play into English verse has been very efficiently performed."—*Graphic.*

Within an Ace. A Story of Russia and Nihilism. By MARK EASTWOOD. Crown 8vo, picture boards, price 2s. ; cloth extra, 3s. 6d. Postage, 4½d.

"Is an exciting and well-written story by one who evidently knows Russia and Russian ways. . . . Most interesting, and we recommend the book as one of the best of its class we have recently come across. The author can tell a story, and he knows his ground so well that his characters and scenes are true to life and nature."—*Pictorial World.*

In Other Lands. By CAROLINE GEAREY, Authoress of "French Heroines," and "Daughters of Italy." Crown 8vo, cloth extra, price 3s. 6d. Postage, 3d.

"Is a charming book of travels."—*Morning Post.*

"A pleasantly written book of reminiscences of foreign travel."—*England.*

Two Daughters of One Race. By C. H. DOUGLAS. Crown 8vo, cloth extra, price 3s. 6d. Postage, 3d.

"The author of this book has produced an interesting story. The quiet, natural style of the writer is a refreshing change from some of the feverish literature of the day."—*Publishers' Circular.*

Saved by a Looking Glass. By EDGAR H. WELLS. Crown 8vo, cloth extra, price 3s. 6d. Postage, 3d.

"Mr Wells tells a startling story in a straightforward manner, that is a strong point in its favour. The crime on which it turns is committed at sea, and surrounded with a singular as well as novel mystery. Suspicion until the last is cleverly diverted from the really guilty man, who is unmasked by a *coup de théâtre* that is certainly dramatical."—*Morning Post.*

Rural Amenities of a Village Community. By WILLIAM J. LOMAX, B.A., St John's College, Camb., and Middle Temple, London. Profusely illustrated with original drawings. Crown 8vo, cloth extra, picture cover. Price 3s. 6d.

"Very amusing. The book is illustrated by a profusion of woodcuts, the designs for which show much vigour and a keen appreciation of the ridiculous. A volume to be taken up at odd times, and enjoyed over a pipe or a cigar."—*Western Daily Mercury.*

My Childhood in Australia. A Story for my Children. By Mrs F. Hughes. Beautifully illustrated throughout with original drawings by the Author. Crown 8vo, cloth extra, price 2s. 6d. Postage, 3d.   [*Just Published.*

Pen and Ink Sketches from Naples to the North Cape. By EMILY A. RICHINGS, Authoress of "Rambling Rhymes," and "Under the Shadow of Etna." Crown 8vo, cloth extra, price 2s. 6d. Postage, 3d.

"I congratulate Miss Emily A. Richings on her little book. . . . The sketch of the blue grotto of Capri is particularly well written, but the chapters on 'Milan,' 'Pisa,' 'St Peter's at Rome,' 'An Alpine Ascent,' and 'A Picnic in Sweden,' will serve to call up pleasant memories to many, and to others an ambition towards greater enterprise in their holiday jaunts."—*Star.*

Waiting for the Dawn. By C. M. KATHERINE PHIPPS. Author of "The Sword of de Bardwell," "Who is the Victor?" and "Douglas Archdale." Crown 8vo, cloth extra, price 2s. 6d. Postage, 3d.

"A pretty, graceful little story have we here, full of humane feeling, and impregnated with genuine piety. There are touches in it which reveal a considerable reserve of literary force in the authoress."—*People.*

Scenes in the Life of a Sailor. By LAWRENCE CAVE. Crown 8vo, cloth extra, price 2s. 6d. Postage, 3d.

"The story of his engagement and the account of the wedding are prettily told."—*Saturday Review.*

Only a Fisher Maiden. By A. MACKNIGHT. Crown 8vo, cloth extra, price 2s. 6d. Postage, 3d.

"The author tells the story with commendable delicacy, and there are passages of genuine pathos."—*Manchester Guardian.*

"A pretty, pathetic story, written in simple language, and most readable."—*Dundee Courier.*

A Child's Solar System, Planets, Comets, Meteors and Falling Stars. With numerous Explanatory Diagrams. By A. B. OAKDEN. Cloth extra, price 1s. Postage, 1½d.

". . . In matter it is simple and plain, and there is no reason why it should not be a permanent possession."—*National Observer.*

18 Bouverie Street, Fleet Street, London, E.C.

Eric Rotherham. By Mrs WILLIAM D. HALL, Author of "Marie." Crown 8vo, cloth extra, price 6s. Postage, 4½d.

"It is a story which can be read and enjoyed. It is graced with some pretty groupings, many pleasing incidents, and not a few well-drawn word pictures and character-sketches."—*Liverpool Post.*

Bairnie. By L. LOBENHOFFER, Author of "Fritz of the Tower," "Theodor Winthrop," etc. Crown 8vo, cloth extra, price 6s. Postage, 4½d.

" Is in point of style and workmanship above the average of many more pretentious works. The characters very well drawn. . . . So distinct and true to life."—*Standard.*

Mrs Danby Kaufman of Bayswater. By Mrs MARK HERBERT. Crown 8vo, cloth extra, price 6s. Postage, 4½d.

·' We found ourselves reading it from beginning to end without any ailure of interest."—*Spectator.*

" Is cleverly written."—*Vanity Fair.*

" Exhibits considerable originality of conception."—*Academy.*

Three Friends. By YRLA. Crown 8vo, cloth extra, price 6s. Postage, 4½d.

" The author may be congratulated on his success in producing a very readable story."—*The Times.*

·· The friends of the title are three Prussian officers during the time of the wars with Napoleon early in the century, and they go through a number of surprising adventures, which are certainly told with spirit."—*Queen.*

The Sandcliff Mystery. By SCOTT GRAHAM, Author of "The Golden Milestone," " A Bolt from the Blues," etc. Crown 8vo, cloth extra, price 6s. Postage, 4½d.

" The tale has some decidedly good things in it in the way of strong situations and epigrammatic comments."—*Athenæum.*

" There is plenty of literary ability distributed over ' The Sandcliff Mystery.' . . . Its author, indeed, commands an easy style, as ' The Golden Milestone ' proved clearly enough, and has rather a turn for sarcasm."—*Academy.*

The Kisses of an Enemy. By MARY SMITH. Crown 8vo, cloth extra, price 6s. Postage, 4½d.

" The characters are realistic, and the book, which gathers in interest with every page, should be read with pleasure by all novel lovers."—*Hereford Times.*

Mrs Lincoln's Niece. By ANN LUTTON, Author of " Whispers from the Hearth." Crown 8vo, cloth extra, price 6s. Postage, 4½d.

" . . . This moving story."—*Academy.*

" This is a story full of thrilling situations. Miss Lutton may be congratulated on the ingenuity she displays in the weaving of her plot. There is some good character-sketching."—*Western Daily Mercury.*

18 Bouverie Street, Fleet Street, London, E.C.

Otho; or, Clasped by a Topaz and a Pearl. By Mrs JANATTA LETITIA BROWN. Crown 8vo, cloth extra, price 6s. Postage, 4½d.

"Well conceived and very well told. . . . Told in a crisp and spirited style."—*Scotsman.*

"Mrs Brown's work is creditably done."—*Pictorial World.*

For the Good of the Family. By KATE EYRE, Author of "A Step in the Dark," "A Fool's Harvest," "To be Given Up," etc. Crown 8vo, paper cover, price 1s.

"It is a prettily written love story."—*Scotsman.*

"Far above the average. It is a lively, pleasant, clever story, and worthy of the author of 'A Fool's Harvest."—*Newcastle Chronicle.*

"A place among entertaining novelette may be freely accorded to Miss Eyre's 'For the Good of the Family.' "—*Academy.*

In Vain. By EDITH HENDERSON, Author of "A Human Spider." Crown 8vo, paper cover, price 1s. Postage, 2d.

"The main incidents are ingenious, and we do not remember to have met with their like before. The story will wile away a passing hour very pleasantly."—*Academy.*

A Family Tradition, and other Stories. By Lady MABEL EGERTON. Foolscap 8vo, paper cover, price 1s.; cloth extra, 1s. 6d. Postage, 2d.

"This volume of tales is from first to last pleasing. Many of them are marked by genuine feeling and pathos."—*Morning Post.*

Up Stream and About Town. A Book for the Summer Holidays. By A BOATING MAN. Picture cover, price 1s. Postage, 2d.

"An amusing little book. The author has the requisite sense of humour, and his record is brightly written."—*Daily Graphic.*

"A series of brightly written and amusing papers. This is just the sort of book for an idle afternoon up the river."—*Lock to Lock Times.*

My Vicars (Second Edition). By A CHURCHWARDEN. Picture cover, price 1s. Postage, 2d.

"A book in which much that is amusing is mingled with much that is profitable. Written in a most appreciative spirit of loyalty to his mother Church, and he will be found to be very interesting and well worth pondering."—*Church Review.*

Honoured by the World. By EMILY FOSTER, Author of "Victims to Custom," "The Folks of Fernleigh," etc., etc. Crown 8vo, paper cover, 1s. Postage, 2d. [*Just Published.*

18 Bouverie Street, Fleet Street, London, E.C.

www.ingramcontent.com/pod-product-compliance
Lightning Source LLC
Chambersburg PA
CBHW022344020726
47500CB00004B/1273